To Elsie and Mike

All the best always

Antoinette

SIREN SHORE THE ENCHANTMENT OF NAPLES

By Antoinette Carone

Except for "The Mayor of Piazza Bellini," the stories contained in his book are all works of fiction. Names, characters and incidents are all products of the author's imagination. Any resemblance to actual persons, living or dead, is entirely coincidental.

Printed in the United States of America at, Shakespeare & Co., 939 Lexington Avenue, New York, NY 10065.

First Edition

978-1-951121-09-9

Other books by the Same Author

Ciao, Napoli, A Scrapbook of Wandering in Naples

Charlie and the Dreadful Mildew

"The Mayor of Piazza Bellini" originally appeared in *Ciao, Napoli, A Scrapbook of Wandering in Naples.*

"The Eternal Return" was originally published in the May 2018 issue of *Ovunque Siamo,* www.ovunquesiamo.com.

"The Guardian Demon" was originally published as "The Demon" in the January 2019 issue of *Ovunque Siamo.*

Antoinette Carone was born in West Virginia. Her father's family originated in the Cilento region of Campania, Italy. She has studied theater in New York city and holds a bachelor's degree in Romance Languages.

When she and her husband decided to spend a year in Naples, she kept a journal which was later published as *Ciao, Napoli -- A Scrapbook of Wandering in Naples.* She is an active member of the New York Writers' Coalition. She maintains a blog: italianscrapbook.wordpress.com.

She now divides her time among New York City; Long Island; and Naples, Italy.

Table of Contents

Introduction

Love and loss, these two oppositions encompass the meaning of being alive, especially in Naples. Joy and Sorrow abound, while underlying the contrasts evident in this city, is a passion for life.

Before Naples was Roman (or Italian), it was Greek. The original name of the city was Partenope, so called for the siren who had loved too well. She had attempted to lure Ulysses to her as he passed through the Mediterranean on his homeward odyssey. He did not return her affection, and in despair she drowned herself. The first Greek colonists found her body on the Island of Megaride where it had washed ashore, in the what is now the Bay of Naples. They buried her nearby on Pizzafalcone Hill and named their newly established colony Partenope in her honor. The roadway that runs along this stretch of the lungomare *today is called Via Partenope.*

Thus, from its very beginnings, Naples has been beset by contradictions – deep caring and profound loss. Life here is ruled by circumstance and fate. But one always meets sympathetic souls who will do what they can to help you along the way. Naples is a special place for those who take the time to explore and to attempt to learn this mysterious city. My husband Jim and I have spent much time in Naples, and still, we do not know everything there is to know. Each time we visit we discover something new.

The stories in this book were inspired by our experiences there. I hope to speak to the depth of feeling, the workings of fortune and the unquenchable joy of life, we have seen in Naples

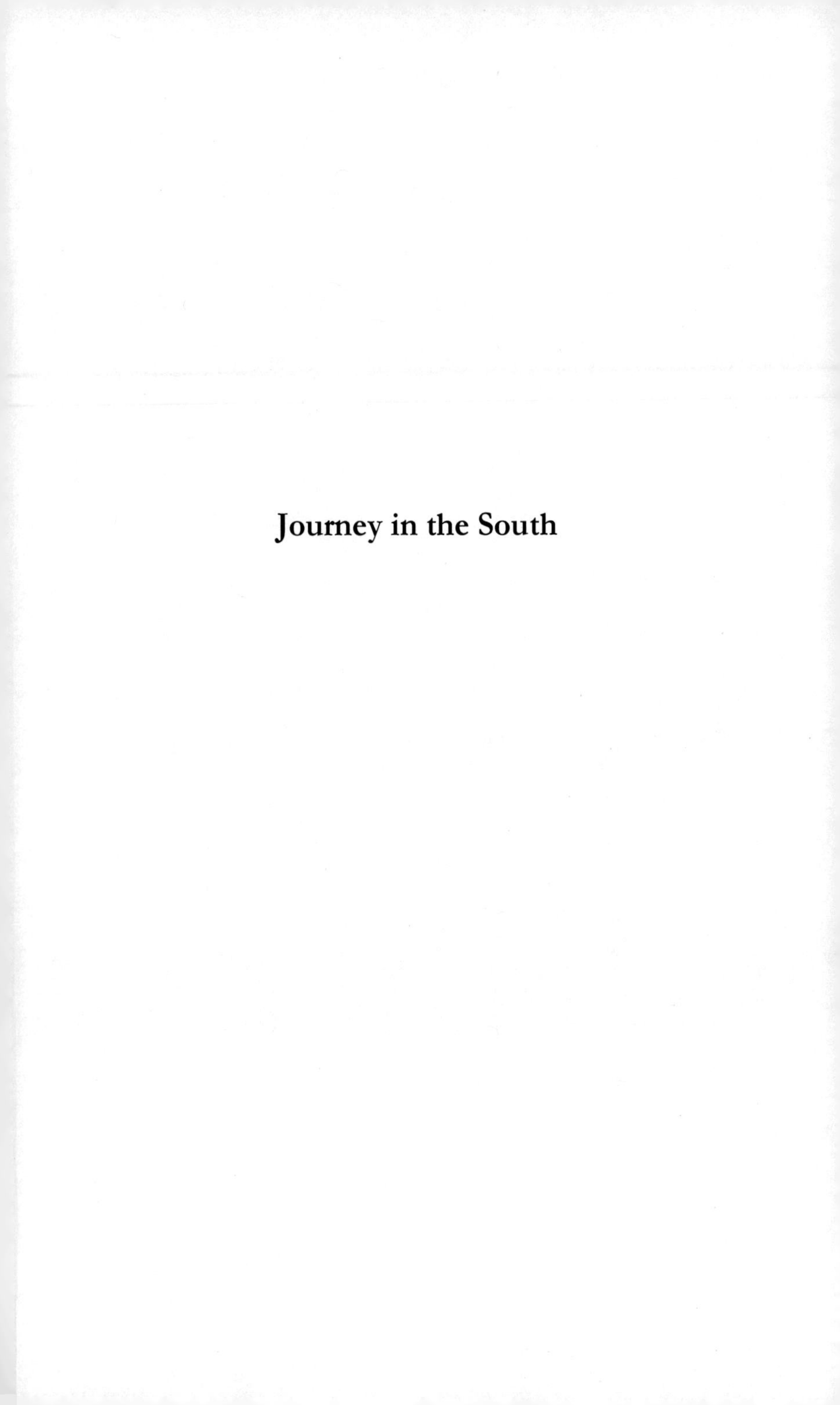

Journey in the South

Naples, Centro Storico

In this one you're smiling – almost smirking, saluting the photographer (me) with your expresso cup. You were happy that day in the Historic Center. We wandered through the ancient city. Movement helped dissipate the tension between us. The sight of ruined walls – fragments of ancient Greece – distracted you.

You picked up a piece of stone that had crumbled from the fortification, tested its weight in your hand, scrutinized its texture between your fingers, then popped it into your bag as a souvenir. I remember thinking that when we get back to our hotel you will label it, record the time, date and place you discovered it, then you will include it as a Greek specimen to add to your Phoenician and Roman artifacts collected in Sardinia. You think quantitatively. You take comfort in what you can measure, what you are certain can be known.

We came upon an open-air market in front of the church San Paolo Maggiore. People were crying out their wares – necklaces of local stone, hand-crocheted bed covers and table runners. All lovely. I wanted one, but you turned away to talk to a dealer in cutting implements. Your Italian had improved, and he knew some English, so you both enjoyed yourselves. You ended up with a very functional pocketknife.

The effort tired you, so on our way back to our apartment on Via Roma, we stopped at an outdoor café for an expresso. You looked so pleased with yourself that I took up the camera and snapped your photo. I think you were even pleased with me as well.

"It's rarely like this nowadays," I thought. "I want to remember this moment."

You caught my desire and toasted me with your expresso. I started to remind you that it is contrary to custom in Italy to make a toast with a non-alcoholic beverage, but then I remembered you had ordered a shot of Sambuca and added it to your expresso. I imagined that made it all right.

I want to remember that day, that desire, that comradery. Memory is so devious, though. It shifts with desire so that what I recall may not be true. Memory may make a liar of me.

Palinura

There was hardly ever a variation in the tide at Palinura, a two-hour drive from Naples, where you had a summer home on the Tyrrhenian Sea. You brought me there in May, at the end of the academic year. We stayed until September. Then we went every weekend until the rains came, even though your house was on a hill rising off the beach, safe from the high waves brought by the rains of November. See, I do remember.

The water was constantly a clear aquamarine. We swam every day for the long period that we stayed there. Looking back, it seems that we were lovers for a long time.

I remember Palinura through its scents. As we would descend the mountain, just before coming up against the blazing white stucco wall that surrounded your house, I could smell the sea. It never gave off that fishy aroma of spent love that the Atlantic (where I grew up) offers at low tide. Nor is it brutal, as the Atlantic can be. The Tyrrhenian Sea is always calm, concealing its promised caresses.

You fascinated me. You were gentle and somewhat of a mystery. Too good to be true and you know the common wisdom of that saying. For my part, I was at my most beautiful from the time I was twenty-eight, until I was thirty-five. My seven years of good luck.

Every May we would open the house in Palinura by placing pots of rosemary along the terrace. When the wind blew in from the sea, the house would vibrate with an herbal and salty smell. Next came the oleander and we would awake to splashes of bright pink and violet. You always made coffee first thing in the morning. The aroma of freshly brewed expresso and steaming milk mingled with that of salt air and rosemary is to me the most exotic of smells.

Another piece of conventional wisdom: nothing lasts forever. The perfume of Palinura would change toward the end of October. The rosemary would wither and lose its fragrance. The sea breeze would blow cold and cause the oleander to pull into itself, hiding its vivid blossoms.

One October you grew tired of me. You kept it to yourself until after Christmas. What a lovely gift! Had you thought you could spare me a lonely holiday? In January you told me you had found someone else. I wasn't surprised. You had been distant that last summer and your smell – your personal odor that only I could sense – had changed. It was no longer like pure dry red wine, but now had a lingering bitter undertone.

I miss the smells of summer – the salty air, wafting rosemary, our excited perspiring bodies, fresh coffee afterward. I live with sterility now. My sheets smell of laundry detergent, my apartment of furniture polish. I have a cat, but it is an odorless animal and I clean the litter twice a day.

I still wonder what turned you away from me. Perhaps you were merely bored? I should now hate the smell of coffee because it always brings to mind the image of you carrying a tray of expresso to the bedroom. I somehow can't obliterate this happy memory that invades me every time I pass a café.

Atrani

On the last day of your life you invited me for coffee. You had seemed to perk up and I had hopes that you had begun to recover. I thought the warm May breeze to be restorative and that you were getting ready to emerge from your winter lair.

Living in Atrani is difficult in the harsh rainy weather that plagues the Amalfi Coast from November through April. I didn't blame you for not wanting to see anyone – for not wanting to see me. You had Maria to clean and cook. You had your records, still preferring vinyl to cd's or even cassettes. What were you reading now? Oh! All the Russian novels! These resonated with your wintery fatalistic mood that you had not yet shed, although the air was mild and bright red flowers covered your terrace. And again, the rosemary.

Now that the weather was warm and dry, I climbed the 50 or so steps from the coastal road in Amalfi and walked the mile or so of tunnel that led into Atrani. Then up up, up, up the side of the mountain I went until I reached your terrace and your little white square stucco house at the far end. You had Maria serve us expresso and lemon torte on the terrace where we could watch the turquoise sea. You played *Largo al Factotum* on your old record player. You offered to be my factotum – something you would not have done in the old days – and we danced a jig to the repetitions of "*di qualitá …di qualitá…di qualitá,"*, the repetitions of the lyric hinting at a corresponding reprise of our present and past mirth.

We talked until the sky turned from a cloudless bright blue to luminescent rose. What was the saying about a "red sky at night brings delight?" Then it gradually faded to violet that merged with the indigo of the evening sea. We talked – and this had never been our custom – about the past and why we couldn't stay together. I left.

The next afternoon Maria called to say that you had died during the night. Of heart failure. Your heart had failed to hold me. But I am grateful for that last day. The enchanting aroma of coffee will never fail to take me back to that long-ago time in Naples when you saluted me with your expresso. And the beguiling colors of that fading day – turquoise, rose, and violet will always by my colors of joy.

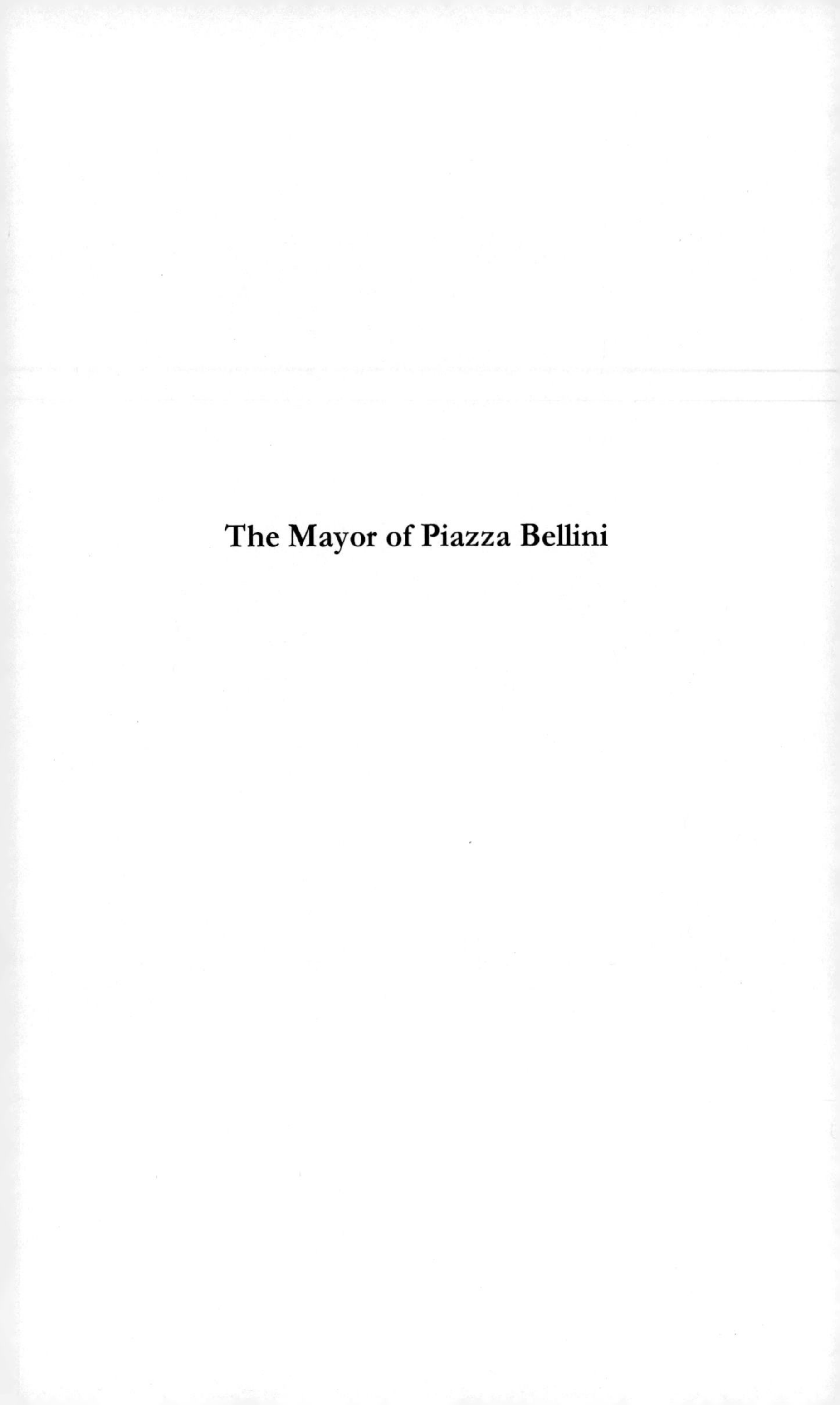

The Mayor of Piazza Bellini

When we lived in Naples, every now and then we would have a cappuccino or espresso at Café Fiorillo on Via Costantinopoli across from Piazza Bellini. Here we would chat with the owner, Vincenzo, who ran the café along with his son Roberto and grandchildren. Vincenzo knew some English, and we knew some Italian, so among us we managed to carry on a pleasant conversation. Here we also became acquainted with Pluto, who lived at Café Fiorillo.

He was sixteen years old, and he carried himself with great dignity. His hair was white with brown spots. He must have been beautiful when he was a puppy. Pluto always crossed Via Costantinopoli slowly and carefully to avoid traffic. He did not so much dodge the *motorini* as make sure the drivers saw him and stopped to let him pass. In his old age, he trembled as he walked. Once in the piazza, the old dog would sniff the periphery of the ancient Greek walls that were exposed below the street level, looking for any tidbits of food that he might like to eat. Then he would lie down in the sunlight, close by the ruins. If a stray dog approached, Pluto would challenge him, rising shakily and growling softly. The young stray seemed to feel some respect for the ancient dog standing before him. He would not growl in return but would lower his head and wag his tail. Then the stray would move on, well-aware that Pluto was the mayor of Piazza Bellini.

We first noticed Pluto when we were passing by on our way through an ancient gate on Via Port'Alba. Pluto was standing beside the table of an elderly gentleman who was enjoying his cappuccino and *cornetto*, the Italian version of a croissant, at Café Fiorillo. Pluto and the gentleman were engaged in a staring contest, but it wasn't a fair contest, as the dog was too much of a match for the man. Pluto had decided he would like some *cornetto* too, so he stood looking at it hopefully, wagging his tail ever so gently, his light brown muzzle only slightly resting against the edge of the table. His eyes were bright, his expression hopeful. Very soon, the gentleman broke off the crispy end and held it out to Pluto, who lay down and ate it slowly.

Although Pluto was in the habit of conning food from the patrons of Café Fiorillo he would decline to eat it if it was not to his liking. Then he would make his way up Via Costantinopoli to a trendy new restaurant, La Stanza del Gusto. This restaurant is not so much like the traditional Neapolitan eating places, but one that would not be out of place in the most upscale neighborhood of New York, one that serves wonderfully tasty cheeses and upscale versions of typical southern Italian cuisine. The owner, Mario, knew Pluto and his mendacious ways. He never offered Pluto anything to eat, so it was then that Pluto would make his way slowly and carefully to Piazza Bellini, where he could scrounge in the Greek ruins.

We went to Café Fiorillo upon our return to Naples one spring. Vincenzo remembered us, of course. Americans in Naples are always noticeable—by sight as well as by their accents. They are the ones who gaze in awe at the works of art that are everywhere on the streets of Naples and which for Neapolitans are a part of everyday life; or they are the ones who look about nervously, convinced that they are going to be accosted and robbed imminently.

Unfortunately, we did not find Pluto at Café Fiorillo; Vincenzo told us that he had died the previous November. At nearly eighteen years old, Pluto's timing had failed. He was hit by a car while crossing Via Costantinopoli on his way to his haunt on the piazza. He is much missed by the patrons of the café. As for us, Pluto will always be the mayor of Piazza Bellini.

Nonna Rosalia

My friend Anna was born in Naples toward the end of World War II. Her family, however, had come from the countryside in the Cilento region about fifty miles southeast of Naples. We became friends in college, and I have never tired of hearing her tell stories of the "old country".

Anna's grandmother Rosalia had lived and died in a small village on the peak of a mountain in the region known as the Cilento, which to this day remains untouched by modernity.

During the World War II, the village never felt the boots of Nazi soldiers climbing its narrow and winding pathways, nor did its inhabitants taste the chocolate offered by American GI's after the Allies' liberation of Italy in 1943. Life continued as it had for centuries past. At sunrise the *contadini* descended the mountain peak to the flatter valley where they worked their fields. They made their own wine and pressed their own olive oil. Families raised sheep, goats, and chickens, so they had plenty of eggs, milk, and cheese. They even had meat for feast days. People lived much as they had since the days of the Romans. Indeed, the *contadini* claimed that their village existed even before the Romans came down to the Cilento to make war with the local tribes. This village was one of the independent mountaintop communities of the region and maintained what we would now call folk ways.

The church was, of course, the center of village life, standing in the piazza at the top of the mountain. The populace faithfully attended mass on Sundays and feast days, but the priests had never quite succeeded in replacing folk traditions with church doctrine. In fact, many priests had no wish to do so, as they themselves came from these traditions. There was one villager, however, who attended church for appearance's sake only. She was a practitioner of the religion of the first inhabitants of the village, those who had preceded the Romans. The secrets of the ancient belief rested within the family and were passed from mother to oldest daughter since time out of mind. No one would remember nowadays of course when the family became ostensibly Catholic, but for centuries it had been wise for members to appear at Sunday mass.

Nonna Rosalia was the village Strega whose understanding of the properties of herbs and their power to heal or to poison brought the villagers to her door. Nonna Rosalia would pour them a glass of wine, listen and propose a solution. Villagers noticed that no rosary was involved in Nonna Rosalia's incantations, nor was there displayed in her home the requisite votive candle and icon of St. Anthony. The villagers did not mind; Nonna Rosalia's spells were effective. Her most important role, however, was to predict the future.

When Nonna Rosalia's daughter, Anna's mother Marialena, was twenty years old, she fell in love with a boy from the village. This was to be expected, of course, since to reach the closest town one had to make one's serpentine way down the mountain, cross the valley and ascend the next mountain. Families married within the village. And so, Giuseppe came courting. Every Sunday he joined the family for the lunch that Nonna

Rosalia and Marialena had prepared, almost as a member of the family. Thus, he learned that Marialena was a good cook and knew how to keep house. And, more important to Rosalia, she could see if he conducted himself as he should – that he made the *bella figura*.

Giuseppe was very well behaved. He always shook hands all around when he came for Sunday lunch and again when he left for the evening. One day, when he shook Nonna Rosalia's hand she felt a cold wave that moved from her fingertips to her shoulder blades. The next morning Nonna Rosalia began to prepare Marialena for sorrow.

"Giuseppe is a nice boy," she said.

Marialena too had felt the cold when Giuseppe had shaken hands good-by with her. "And so?" she asked.

"He will not be with us long," Nonna Rosalia replied. "You will marry, but later. When the war is over." It was 1938.

"I do not understand," said Marialena, although she did. "There is no war now."

In 1939 Giuseppe was drafted into the Italian army. In 1940 he was sent to the Russian front. Marialena, when she learned of this, went to her grandmother's closet, took out one of her black dresses and put it on. Nonna Rosalia insisted that she not wear black because, "It would take hope away from Giuseppe's parents." Marialena understood and complied, but she made herself a handkerchief from a piece of black cloth which from then on, she carried concealed in her pocket.

A year later, Giuseppe's mother came to visit Nonna Rosalia. After Nonna Rosalia had poured the wine and sat down to listen, Giuseppe's mother asked if Nonna Rosalia could tell her where he was or if he were even still living. Nonna Rosalia was compassionate. She said that he was dead, killed instantly from a gunshot. He had not suffered. Rosalia could not find it in her heart to tell about the terrible cold she had felt when she and Giuseppe shook hands, nor did she mention that she had sensed the cold of the Russian winter, nor the slow decomposition of the living body that begins with frostbitten toes.

Poor Man, Rich Man

"Poor man, rich man, beggar man, thief," I sang as my grandmother unbuttoned my coat. It had four buttons. "Does that mean I am going to marry a thief when I grow up?"

"No," said Nonna. "Maybe you will marry a rich man."

"A thief could be rich," I answered lapsing into the dialect I used with my grandmother and sometimes my mother.

"You don't have to marry a man who is rich," continued Nonna in dialect. "You could be rich yourself."

I thought about what my grandmother had said as I curled up on the sofa where she had taken up her knitting. We were both tired after a morning spent in the park.

"Tell me a story -- a true one."

"A true one? About what?"

"About someone who was rich. A lady who got rich," I answered.

"Hmmm. *Allora*, my mother – your great-grandmother – was always afraid of being poor.

"Why?"

"Her family worked very hard to make a living. However, her father always talked about the time that Naples was rich, when it was ruled by the king."

"What happened to the king?"

"He went to live with the Pope when all the parts of Italy were joined together to make one big nation. Then all the wealth of the Kingdom of Naples was given to the whole country. The people from the south, where we come from, became very poor. Still, the family owned land and raised sheep and rabbits and grew enough *verdure* to set a very nice table. -- Do you remember where I lived when I was a little girl?"

"Yes, Nonna. In a village in Naples."

"It was not a village, but a part of the big city of Naples. It was called Poggioreale. Many, many years ago, there was a grand villa on the hill of Poggioreale, but now there is only a graveyard. When I was a little girl, and even before that when my mother was a young woman, there were fields where we could grow vegetables and raise sheep."

"Did your mother get rich there?" I asked.

"In a way."

"What way?"

"You'll see. When my mother was eighteen years old, she was what Italians call 'nubile' which only means 'ready for marriage'. To acknowledge this, she insisted on being called Regina instead of just Gina and she began to behave in a queenly manner. There were few young men in Poggioreale that she approved of," my grandmother went on, "so she began to go with her father on Saturdays to the market in Sanità in the middle of Naples, where he would sell sheep's milk cheese and the ricotta his wife made."

"Were they rich?"

"No, but they were not poor either. And, Regina – my mother -- was skilled at needlework. She was known for her lace and had edged the linens and earned money for the family by making trousseaux for families living nearby. Regina had made several white muslin blouses and worked various lace patterns for bodices, collars and cuffs to take to the market with her. She hoped to be able to sell these as well as the ricotta.

"Regina and her father would leave early on Saturday mornings. They walked a long way from their house to the marketplace in Sanità. Their donkey pulled a cart laden with good things made from sheep's milk, but Regina carried her wares on her head."

"Why?"

"So she could walk for long distances without tiring her arms or shoulders. That was how all the women in that time carried baskets of fruit and vegetables. Her mother had taught her how to coil fabric to cushion the weight and help hold it up

"Regina and her father, who was my grandfather Nonno Vito, well, they would make their way to a big street called Via

Foria where they would pass an enormous building called *Albergo dei Poveri*, which was a home for poor people to live in.

"This place always frightened Regina because Nonno Vito would say each time they passed, 'You see this great palace? Over two-hundred years ago a good king of Naples started to build it. All the poor people, not only in city of Naples but in the whole kingdom, were supposed to live there.'

"Regina would cross herself as they passed. She felt sorry for the poor people who lived there because her father said that the *Albergo* was now more prison than shelter. Regina hoped that she would never have to go there.

"Finally, they would see the Port of San Gennaro in the old city wall and know they had arrived at the marketplace in Sanità. Regina would help her father set up their stall. His space was next to that of Signore Pasquale who was a silversmith. Signore Pasquale operated a small shop near the train station during the week, but he also came to the market on Saturdays.

"In fact, everybody came to Sanità on Saturdays. The rich people sent their servants, for they would never allow themselves to be seen there. Only poor people lived in Sanità."

"What were the rich peoples' servants doing there if it was a market for poor people?"

"Well, they say that the best markets are found in poor neighborhoods. But, Sanità was once the part of Naples where nobility lived," Nonna explained. "When the rich people moved away, only poor people were left."

"Why did the rich people move away?"

"Sanità is in a valley and you had to pass through it to get to the royal palace. Then bridge was built over the valley, so nobody went to Sanità anymore. The grand *palazzi* were abandoned. When they walked through the marketplace Regina and Nonno Vito would pass by grand old *Palazzo San Felice* or *Palazzo Spagnolo*. Regina was my mother, remember. When I was a little girl, she told me often how their vanished elegance never failed to disturb her."

I thought about this. I couldn't form the words at the time, but I now realize I felt that perhaps this too made Regina afraid of being poor. Fortunes always seemed to change in my grandmother's stories. I could see why it might be better to marry a wealthy man.

"So how did your Mamma Regina get rich? I asked. "Did she want to marry a rich man?"

"Yes, she did," Nonna said. "She kept looking around the marketplace for a man who was rich and handsome. Naples is a big port. Soldiers and sailors roamed the marketplace searching for gifts to send back home. Sometimes a soldier or a sailor would buy some lace or an embroidered handkerchief from Regina. They looked handsome in their uniforms, but Regina wasn't sure if they would make good husbands."

"So how did she find a rich husband?"

"Signore Pasquale had recently started to bring his son Giuseppe with him to the market. Beppe was himself a capable craftsman, even better than Signore Pasquale. Beppe quickly fashioned candle holders, bowls, serving platters that filled their stall. Young women about to be married almost always bought one of Beppe's delicate serving dishes or a candle holder or even one of what he called his *objects d'art*."

(Beppe read a lot and had dreams of going to America.)

"Signore Pasquale and Nonno Vito would take turns watching each other's stalls when one of them would need to be absent or when Regina wanted to visit other stalls and her father insisted on accompanying her.

"One day when Regina began to grow restless in the afternoon warmth, her father suggested that they walk through the market. Perhaps she could find fabric or embroidery floss that would please her. Nonno Vito had just that morning taken a commission for a set of bed linens for her to edge and embroider the initials of the bride and groom. They were to be picked up at this stall this time next month, in time for their wedding. In fact, Regina was beginning to bring in a lot of money for the family –

more than the ricotta. As fate would have it, Beppe offered to accompany her instead.

"Regina wondered if Beppe and his family were well off, but not only would it have been improper to ask, no one would have told her the truth anyway: people kept what wealth they had invisible so no one would try to steal it or cheat them out of it. She could only observe. It was just as easy to love a rich man as a poor man; of that she was sure. She would wait and see.

"Regina found that she enjoyed Beppe's company. She told him what her father had said about the ruined *palazzi*. Beppe said that he hoped to go to America where there was no such danger of falling into ruin, especially with his skill as a silversmith. When they returned to their stalls, Beppe was loaded with sewing materials and spices that Regina had purchased from an Arab merchant. Regina was thinking she would ask her father to invite Beppe to dinner, so that she would have good occasion to use these.

"So, for a few months, almost a year maybe, Regina and Beppe would walk through the market and linger in each other's company."

"Was Beppe as handsome as the soldiers and sailors?"

"I think so."

"Was he rich?"

"He made a very good living. But don't forget, my mother was also very skilled at sewing and lacemaking. She also brought in a lot of money for her family."

"Did she marry Beppe and live happily ever after?"

"Let me finish the story. Of course Signore Pasquale and Nonno Vito noticed that Regina and Beppe were falling in love, but Nonno Vito would not allow Regina to invite Beppe to come to dinner. Signore Pasquale was very happy with Regina, for he saw that she made beautiful linens and things and would be a help to his family. But Nonno Vito did not want to lose the money Regina brought in. If she got married, all her money would go to her husband."

"Why couldn't she keep her money?"

"That was in the old country. It's different here in America."

"I think Nonno Vito was mean. Did he ever change his mind?"

"I will tell you. Beppe and Regina decided to marry anyway and come to America. They would walk in the marketplace pretending to look for cloth and thread while making their plans. There is a cemetery a little ways from the marketplace. In that cemetery people are not buried, but their bones rest there. It is made up of great caves with rooms and rooms of bones."

"Was it scary?"

"No, it was peaceful."

"Were there evil ghosts?"

"No, only good souls. Shall I finish the story?"

I nodded, fascinated.

"Well, one day Beppe and Regina were gone for a long, long time. In those days no one looked after the bones in the cemetery, so kind people would visit them, and clean the skulls and light candles for them. In return, the souls that belonged to the bones, would help them."

"They were good ghosts?"

"Not ghosts. Bones that were once people who lived in Naples and now their souls could look down from Heaven. So, Beppe and Regina adopted a skull. They named it Ciro because it was rather large, so they thought it must have been a man in life. They cleaned it and lit a candle beside it. Regina gave it a collar she had embroidered, and Beppe gave it a silver cross. They asked Ciro's soul to help them find a way to get married and go to America."

"Did they?"

"Wait and see. The only person Regina could talk to about her love for Beppe was her grandmother, Nonna Francesca who was Nonno Vito's mother. Regina did not tell of her plans to get married and go to America, but Nonna Francesca understood their love for one another. When she and Regina were alone on Sunday afternoons after lunch, Nonna Francesca would make coffee and they would talk about Beppe. I don't know if these conversations made Regina dream or if Nonna Francesca put some special herbs in her coffee, but something magical happened. Regina did have a dream and she told it to Nonna Francesca.

"'Tell it to your father,' Nonna Francesca said.' And see what happens.'

"'Babbo,' Regina said on their way to market the next Saturday. 'Last night I dreamed about Nonna Francesca. We were in the kitchen and she was serving me coffee. She asked me if I wanted grappa or sugar and I did not know which to accept.'

"'That is a good dream,' replied Nonno Vito. 'I must buy a lottery ticket.'

"Nonno Vito reached into his jacket pocket and pulled out an old booklet. Do you know what it was?"

"No. What was it?"

"It was called the Smorfia. It is a list of things you dream about. Each dream has its own number and if you play these numbers in lotto you can win. Nonno Vito looked at this old thing and said, 'first was Nonna Francesca, yes?'

'Yes,' said Regina.

'Nonna Francesca is an old lady – number 89.'

'Then she was serving coffee. Were you sitting at the table? Was it set with cups and plates?'

'Yes.'

'Good, good. Number 82'

'Then coffee. Number 42. And grappa. A good wine. Number 45'

"So Nonno Vito played 89-82 -42-45. And he won! But that wasn't enough for Nonna Francesca. She told her son that now that he had a fortune of his own, he should be generous enough to allow his daughter to marry."

I was getting impatient and wanted a happy ending.

"Did your Mamma Regina and Beppe ever get married?" I asked.

"Yes. Did you know my real name is Pasqualina, not Patsy? For Beppe's father, Signore Pasquale, my other grandfather."

"And did they come to America and get rich?" I asked.

"They did not come to America. Beppe wanted to and so did Regina, but Signore Pasquale and Nonno Vito both wanted them to stay. Signore Pasquale had a good business, so Beppe was well off. Besides, Nonno Vito said that they must have the courage to stay in Italy and not run away."

I to this day don't know if he was right, but I know that the Neapolitans have always been skilled in the art of "making do". My great-grandmother passed this skill on to my grandmother Pasqualina who in turn passed it on to my mother Giuseppina. (Yes, named after her grandfather Giuseppe who was known to all as Beppe.) More than that, though, my mother had her own fiery spirit.

My family did eventually come to America. My mother was a World War II bride. Her mother, my Nonna Patsy, followed her a few years later, after I was born. My older brother was still small, and my mother needed help. She had a very good part-time job doing alterations on women's dresses in a department store; with two children, the money came in handy. Nonno Beppe had recently passed away and my mother wanted to be among family. Moreover, she wanted her children to know their nonna. It is thanks to Nonna Patsy that I know my old country heritage.

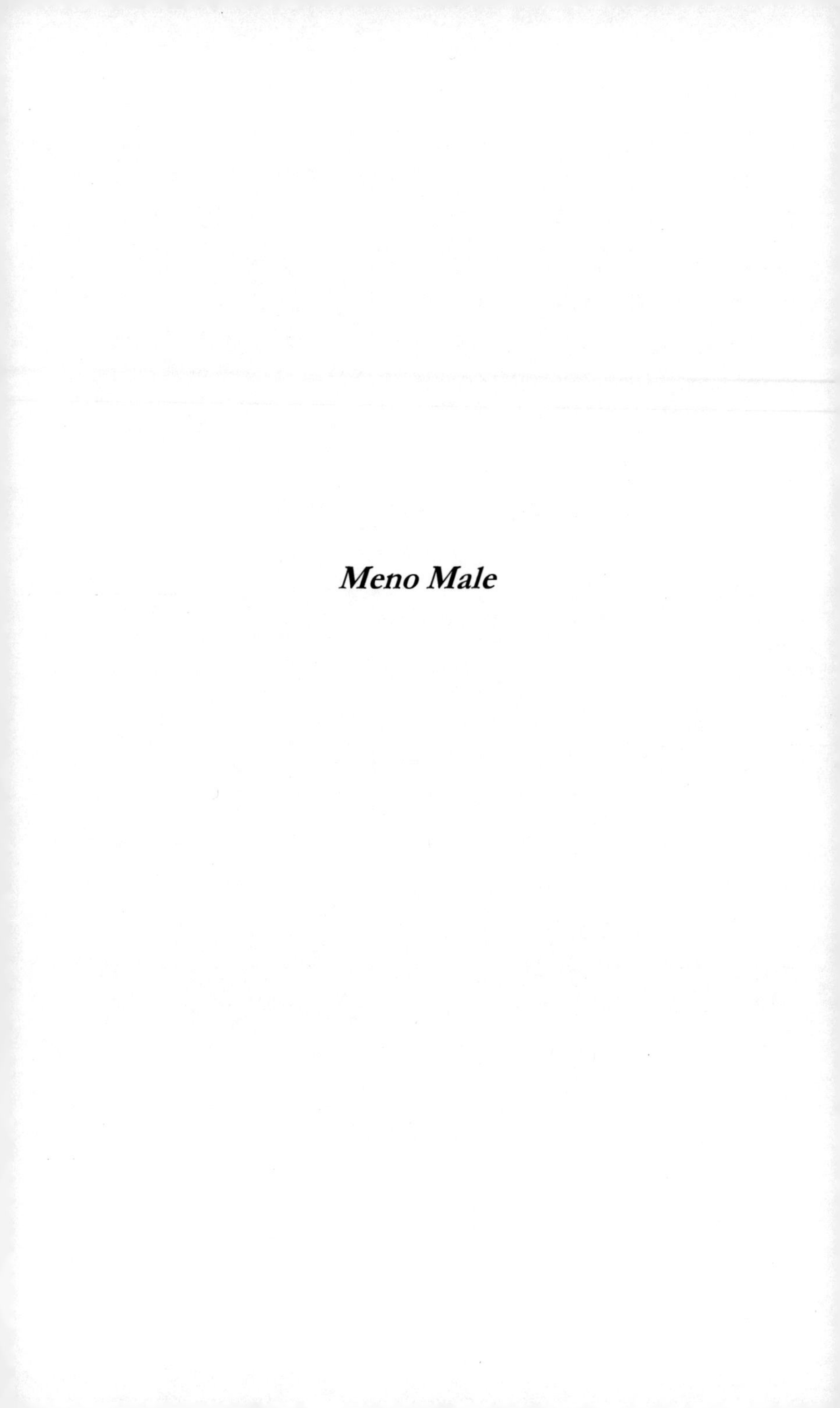

Meno Male

Mario hated his job. He had trained as a mechanic, but was unable to find permanent, full-time work. He was tired of living on unemployment and fixing his friends' broken machinery. Finally the position of attendant at the WC of the *circumvesuviana* train station at Avella became available. Mario put in his application.

"*Meno male. Ho un lavoro.*" he said to himself when he was notified of his hiring. "Not so bad. I have a job."

The station where he worked was the second-to last on the line that linked Avella to Naples. Even though he lamented not doing the work he was trained for, Mario was grateful to have work. His was a government job, which meant that he would have it for the rest of his life. He couldn't be fired, and he couldn't move forward. All day Monday through Friday from 8 am until 4 pm Mario sat in the anteroom between the men's and women's toilets and collected fifty eurocents from anyone wanting to use the facilities.

The system had been in place since the nineteen-thirties when it was installed by the fascists. Since that time, attendants had been taking fifty eurocents (although in those days it was a thousand lire). After paying, the patrons were permitted to go through a turnstile which counted the number of people who went through. The clicks of the turnstile and the coins had to tally. No chance for the attendant to pocket a few extra cents. In the 'thirties, he or she might have been shot for such a crime against the State; nowadays he would be suspended while undergoing a lengthy defense. Finally the government would find that he couldn't be fired for such an insignificant misdemeanor.

Mario wouldn't have pocketed the few cents in any event. He, like a lot of other Italian men who had trained as mechanics, also knew carpentry. "*Meno male*," he would repeat to himself when he found he could spend the time between trains, when he was compelled to remain in front of the toilets, designing machines, His evenings he passed repairing and constructing for friends and friends of friends. He had an income the government didn't know about. He was quasi tax-free.

A lot of Italians contrive to be quasi tax-free, not making the connection to the diminished services provided by the government (although there many levels of fiscal irresponsibility within the government). Around June of each year, the train station's supply of soap and toilet paper would run out. No more would be provided until January when the next year's budget would go into effect. For more than six months Mario would be compelled to listen to complaints of angry patrons about the lack of *carta igenica* and *sapone*. He grew weary of apologizing and sympathizing.

Since he was so mechanically inclined, Mario liked to rummage through garbage dumps to find things to tinker with and repair. On one such excursion he found a coffee vending machine discarded by an office in Ravenna when the administrator had purchased an updated one. Mario's machine, for sixty eurocents each, sold expresso, cappuccino, or hot chocolate. Sugar was free, but there was an extra button for this commodity.

Mario repaired the machine. Then he went to *Spendimeglio* (which means "spend better"), a discount store that sells household products at very good prices. Mario stocked up on toilet paper, soap and hand cream. He rigged up the vending machine to sell a small stock of toilet paper for one euro and soap and hand cream for fifty eurocents each.

He set up the vending machine behind his table in the train station. In June when bathroom provisions ran out, Mario put a sign in front of the machine, indicating that they could be purchased from the machine, so that it didn't appear that he was selling them himself. Nobody cared. Patrons were in fact happy – they needed soap and toilet paper and the quality the machine offered was better than the standard issue. Of course, Mario gave these necessities to his colleagues for free.

"*Meno male*," said Mario to himself again when he was asked if he would take his annual vacation in February instead of August when almost all of Italy goes on vacation. After all, pleaded his superior who planned to go to Florida in August, the station will have to remain open. People will still take trains. February fell during the period when the government-issue soap and toilet paper were still in abundant supply. Mario preferred cold weather and could afford to go to Vermont in the US to ski.

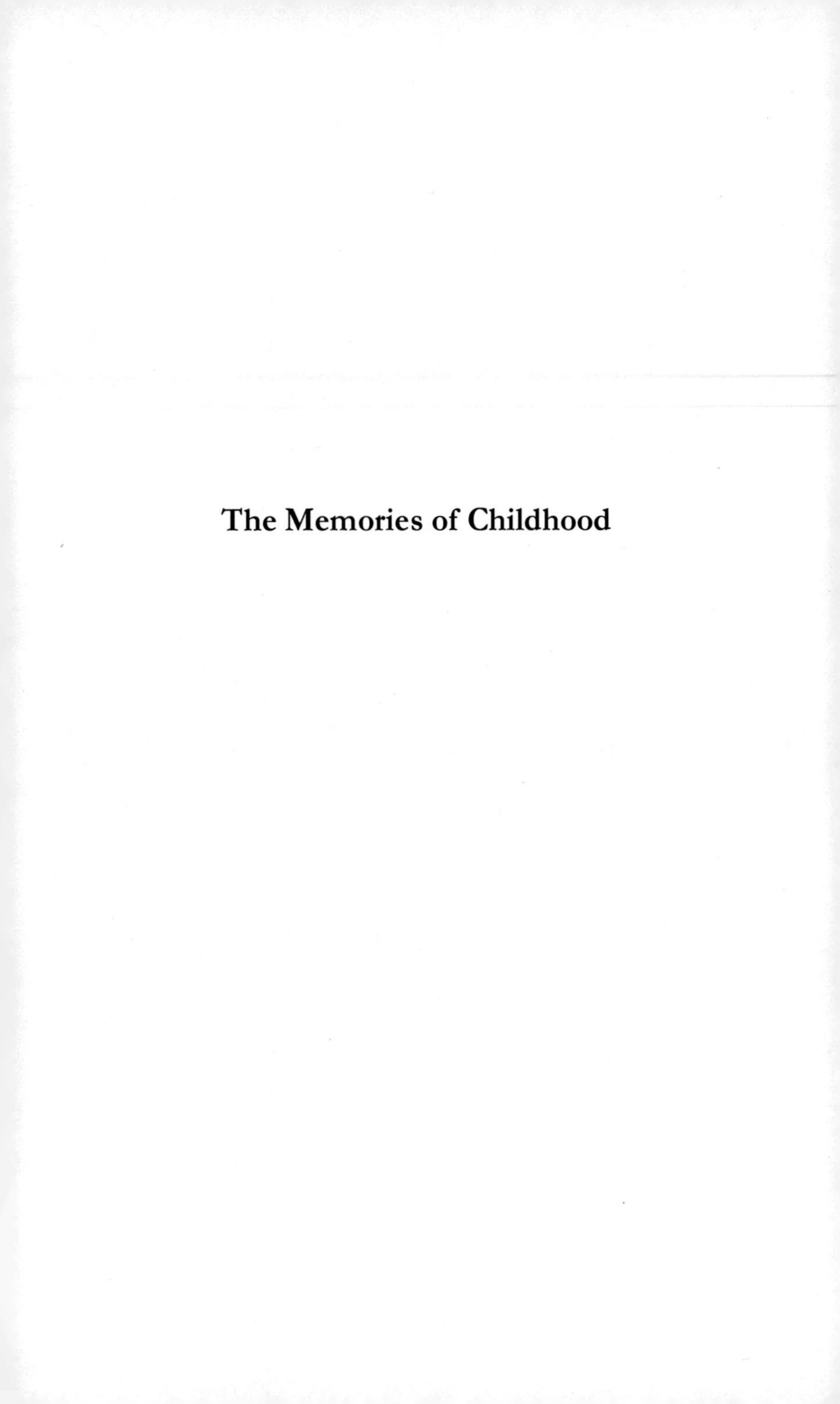

The Memories of Childhood

As I drift off to sleep, I float into a hilly pasture. The air smells of pine, broom and something else – something bodily and perhaps slightly obscene. People are speaking in a language I don't understand. I awake to listen, and the dream is lost.

It was thirty years ago today that my mother died. I had been thinking of her all day. Had she lived she would now be one hundred years old. Sometime during the last week of her life, she forgot English. She could speak only Italian and her dialect at that. Only my brother and I understood her, so we became her translators, telling the doctors what pained her, fulfilling her requests for forbidden foods which we covertly brought to her, but of which she never ate more than a bite. She told us for the last time stories of her youth when she lived just outside of Naples.

Her family lived in a stucco house that lay on the edge of a wide pasture. They were land-rich, but money-poor. They raised sheep and sold the cheese made of their milk to the neighboring village. My mother's brothers took turns staying in the fields at night to throw stones and any wolves that might wander down from the mountains and attempt to carry off one of the sheep. By the time my mother was a young woman, the wolves had been driven even farther south, but memories of ravaged flocks persisted and one or another of my uncles always passed a sleepless night.

Had this been my dream? Had I been re-living the life of the Old Country – a life that, after all, wasn't mine? But I know my mother's native language. Why couldn't I understand what was being said?

The light coming into my bedroom changes from pale to bright. A young woman is in the fields next to the stucco house. She is picking beans. It is wartime. A mounted officer is watching her. She is watching him in return. She becomes aware that she has watched too long and bends over to resume picking. I see the swastika on his uniform as he urges his horse toward her. He bends forward and tries to lift her onto his horse. She slaps him. Realizing what she has done, she steps back horrified. But he is an officer and a gentleman. He apologizes – in German.

I see his face – this handsome German officer. Strong, slightly square jaw, high Eastern European cheekbones, light hair. Probably blond. I really can't tell the color of his hair in the black and white photo. Photo? Yes. I found the photo in the back of my mother's jewelry drawer after she died. There was not a lot of jewelry – a string of pearls, a jet brooch, scatter pins of a snake and a snake charmer. The photo was in the back under the Mother's Day cards my brother and I had made in elementary school. I was touched that she had kept them. The officer in the photo looks like my brother did when he was in his twenties.

In 1943 my mother married an American, my father. It was shortly after the American invasion of Italy as the Allies marched north from Sicily. My brother Carl, or Carlo as she always called him, was born in Italy in 1944. My father marched northward and continued to fight. After the War, he brought my mother and brother to New York where I was born in 1946.

I remember the photo. I had first seen it when I was about five years old.

"Is that my Uncle Vito?" I had asked. I knew about my uncle who had been killed in the war.

"No," my mother answered. "His name was Karl. He was a friend. He was killed too."

Maledetto

The vision took place in the West Fourth Street station – the one where the Sixth Avenue and the Eighth Avenue lines converge, then go their separate ways.

I had no intention of getting off there. I was just passing through on my way to meet Janna at a nouveau foodie restaurant on Spring Street.

I remembered that they don't accept credit cards, but I had already gotten off the LIRR *and made my way into the subway, the Eighth Avenue line and was on the* E *train. I knew that there is a branch of my bank near the West Fourth Street station. Hence my getting off the train at that stop.*

I knew which exit to take – the one on West Third Street. It seemed that the bank was now where O. Henry's Steak House once had been. I had memories of very happy times at O. Henry's Steakhouse with Sebastian, where, ravenous after a performance, I always had a rare sirloin burger – rare, I say, but it was in fact raw in the middle and charred on the surface. Red *wine accompanied it, at least two glasses and sometimes three.*

I married Sebastian in 1969. He was Italian; so we went to live in Naples, a city as ancient and mysterious as he turned out to be. For a while I felt blessed.

*****

The simple pleasure of warm sun. That was what I longed for when the autumn rain began to fall on Naples. The damp penetrated my bones. The chill was unrelenting.

On the last day of October, the pool in the courtyard was drained and covered for the coming winter. It was odd to think that only a few days before, we were still swimming in its balmy water. Even the day before, I had remarked on the trees surrounding the pool – at a respectable distance to avoid a clogging abundance of fallen leaves. I was impressed that these trees still held on to their foliage, so stately and proud. But Sebastian had said one must think ahead and had had the pool drained and covered while I was out shopping.

I had walked down Via Costantinopoli in the stillness of dead and dropping leaves, leaves that had been on the trees yesterday. The sun was out, heating the stones in Piazza Bellini where the old dog from a nearby café lay warming his ancient bones. I made my way to my favorite pastry shop on Via Tribunali where my mouth watered at a display of nougat candy called *torrone* in the window – all different kinds. Vanilla and chocolate, of course; but also green nougat which was pistachio and also coffee nougat. Some with almonds; some with hazelnuts. I had noticed that these confections had appeared in the shops around the beginning of October, along with chestnut gelato. (This I bought for myself every chance I got, since, I had been warned, it was seasonal and would soon disappear.)

When I returned home with a large package of various *torrone*, I found the pool drained and covered. I had hoped for one last swim, but it was not to be. Maria took the package from me, saying it was too heavy.

"Why is there *torrone* only at this time of year?" I asked her.

"It's for the dead," she answered. "The white nougat is molded into a long form and represents the bones of the dead. For us all life, even its end, has meaning,"

Maria then went on to explain that this time of the year holds significance for the end of life. All Saints' Day on November 1st, and All Soul's Day on November 2nd fall exactly between the time of the year when day and night are equal and the time of year when the daylight is shortest. At this time of year, the veil between the worlds of the living and dead was thinnest. On All Saints' Day, we honor the dead who were holy; All Souls' Day we acknowledge all the others who have left life on earth. It is the day on which ordinary people are remembered and prayed for. We want the dead to assist us in life, so we must honor them. The custom of propitiating the dead, she told me, was initiated by Romulus after the founding of Rome. Romulus did not want his brother, with whom he argued then killed, to return and seek vengeance. Autumn can be a malevolent time and we must be cautious.

Sebastian and his family began their festivities on the evening of October 31st. Hallowe'en in my former life. My favorite holiday when I could disguise myself as whatever grabbed my fancy. I had always been attracted to costumes and fantasy. But here in Naples, we spent the day in the *Cimitero Monumentale*, wandering amongst graves and finally visiting the family vault. I did not mind, however. I had found another way of being in the quiet dignity of this place. Just keeping still, letting something happen it its own good time.

Workmen were preparing another vault. For Sebastian and me? There was a third unmarked stone on the ground, so small that I tripped over it while looking at the names in the mausoleum. It seemed ominous at first, but then I considered that I was merely being drawn in by the mood of my surroundings.

Sebastian's mother, Signora Bella, talked about her late husband Gennaro as if he had only just been placed in the mausoleum, whereas he has been there for twenty years. The stone was beginning to wear at Gennaro's name and likeness because Signora Bella had passed her hand over it so often, letting it linger over his face. She never remarried.

La Signora tried to keep close to Sebastian and he did not seem to mind. I sometimes wondered how he ever managed to get away to New York. What must La Signora have thought when he returned with a wife!

Right after All Souls' Day the scirocco came. It started with a few drops of rain. Then wind – in full force. Sebastian had been right about draining the pool. By the afternoon, the trees were completely bare, and the cover was chocked with leaves and red dust. The cars on the street looked as if they had been in a sandstorm. Red dust covered everything, and craters had formed where giant raindrops had landed.

"This is the dust of Africa," Maria told me.

I stayed inside the villa and tried to stay warm. I was tired just waiting. I felt heavier and bigger today. I could hardly move, and nowhere, but nowhere could I find a comfortable spot to just sit.

"Soon," said Maria. "It will be soon."

But it would not be so very soon. Isabella was due on Christmas Day. (Maria had said it would be a girl.) We were hoping she would come early because Christmas Day was Sebastian's birthday. La Signora said that it was a sin to be born on Christ's birthday and the poor creature would suffer just as Sebastian did. I was curious as to what she meant. La Signora, I suspected, had prevailed upon Maria to brew a potion that would make Isabella come ahead of time. I would refuse all drinks that I didn't brew myself until the middle of December, when I felt it would be safe.

To stave off the damp left by the sirocco, I made myself a cup of expresso and arranged a sort of nest of the cushions on the divan. Sebastian brought me a small piece of each of the *torrone* I had bought. As I sipped and sampled, blue seeped through the sky and with it the sunlight. I thought of the next holiday, one that Sebastian and I would celebrate together. I lay back in gratitude for the warmth of both the sun and Sebastian.

I was growing bigger by the day. At the beginning of Advent, Maria felt my belly and assured me and Sebastian that the baby would be born before time, that is before Christmas Day. With Christmas approaching and all the tumult of preparations, I was fortunate to have found a space for myself in the library. The villa was a busy place with all the comings and goings of servants. This was a time of grand dinners, and still Sebastian never seemed to eat much. Family was visiting from the Cilento. The guests were served homemade pasta in fragrant sauces of truffles or eggplant or perhaps lupini clams – all with bits of fresh tomato and garlic and, of course basil and parsley. Sebastian nibbled at these, but when roast beef was passed around, he declined to take any.

Roast beef is rare in this part of the world. Generally, beef here is not tasty. The land is too hilly and rocky to provide good pasture for cows. It is more suitable for sheep and goats who produce great quantities of milk that is made into delectable cheeses, some of which are then sometimes turned into excellent ricotta. Nevertheless, Sebastian had a source for beef -- a friend in Argentina, so the roast beef served at the dinners here was excellent and I thought he should have relished it. But then, I had an almost insatiable desire for meat. Maria encouraged me to eat it, saying that it was good for me now, but perhaps once the baby came, it might not be good for the child. Sebastian had grown up on only fish, cheese and vegetables and had been fine until…. she did not go on. I craved meat and ate as much as I could at these family dinners while Sebastian watched me closely. I couldn't quite decipher his expression which seemed to vary from vexation to tenderness.

On morning of Christmas Eve, I suddenly felt tired and touchy. I wanted to be alone. I wanted to hide from the joyous throng and read in solitude. I slipped away before the *aperitivo* was served and made my way into the library where my quiet alcove awaited. There was quite a collection of books – oddly enough, though, most dated from the nineteenth century. However, there were some contemporary writers – in Spanish, French and German as well as in Italian. I found a book of stories by Primo Levi and started to read "Lilith" but was distracted by a children's book (my condition?), the original "Pinocchio". Two disparate books, but to my mind they found common ground in their vision of desire as a force of evil.

I needed something less profound, so I began to peruse the family Bible for names and birth dates of Sebastian's relatives. I was curious about anything concerning Sebastian. He would never tell me his age. The Bible contained old, old records, but I found an entry for "Sebastian, born 25 December 1899 at the stroke of midnight." There was never any other man with his name in the family. That he did tell me. And it is very unusual in an Italian family that a son is not named for his father or one of his grandfathers. Written in the margin near the entry was a single word – *maledetto*. Cursed.

The next point in time that I can find in my memory I am holding newborn Isabella. Born early the same afternoon – before sunset – on December 24th, she had quieted some vague fear I had sensed in Sebastian and his mother. The baby had come a day early, thanks to Maria's potions. I was touched by the infinite possibilities that lay before Isabella. All of Sebastian's and my cultures combined within her suggested talents beyond belief.

But at a week old, Isabella had stopped sleeping and had begun to fret. This troubled Maria who said that there was still something wild in Isabella's nature and that we must endeavor to tame it. Often when Isabella had been crying for over an hour and I couldn't sooth her, Maria would take her from me. I watched her walking with the baby as I drifted off to sleep. I had observed Maria studying Isabella's tiny hands and feet. What kind of sign was she searching for, I wondered?

Since January in Naples is wet and rainy, I had stayed indoors since Isabella's birth. Even Sebastian's mother, La Signora, had not objected when I declined to go to mass that morning for the Epiphany. Epiphany – when the divine or some mystery is to be revealed. For La Signora it was a Holy Day of Obligation.

"You will receive your revelation in any event," she told me as she set off that damp and chilly morning of January 6th. "I will pray for you."

She looked at Sebastian, but I felt her words were directed to me as well.

"Do you want to accompany your mother?" I had asked Sebastian. "I don't mind."

"I cannot," he replied.

That evening I was feeling mellow and drowsy. Isabella was now a little over two weeks old. She had finally fallen asleep and was lying in the cradle next to my bed. Darkness came early now, bringing Sebastian to my bedside with nightfall. He was happy. He approved of the name I had chosen, which was also his mother's name. Most of all he was happy that Isabella had not been born on Christmas Day as he had.

In the half-light of my consciousness, I asked Sebastian about the birth record I had found and why was there written alongside of it the word *maledetto.*

I am *maledetto.* I was born at midnight on December 25th, just as the church bells were ringing for Midnight Mass. I am cursed because I had the arrogance to be born at the same hour as Christ. One born at such time will turn into a human wolf – or worse."

"But calendars have changed," I objected. "Nowadays scholars don't assign that date to Christ's birthday. And you're not a practicing Catholic."

"It is still a belief in my family's village," Sebastian answered. "The curse was uttered over five-hundred years ago by Maria's ancestor to prove her faith to her torturers during the time of the Inquisition. She was a *strega* and her spells were powerful.

There has always been a *strega* in the village – until recently. No one pays attention anymore, but the power is still there.

*****

When I got off the E train at West Fourth Street, I had a vision of Sebastian standing at the Third Street entrance, as he did long ago. But maybe it was something more substantial. As I approached the stairs, I saw a rat looking at me with sad eyes before he ran away.

Via Partenope

On a warm morning toward the end of October Antonio and Giacomo enjoyed quiet companionship at the café overlooking the sea on Via Partenope. It was a time of solitude that left Antonio, without his being aware of it, open to possibility.

At precisely thirteen minutes past ten, he saw her. She was running along, along the *lungomare,* the Bay of Naples. She was wearing black pants that fit loosely and ended just below the knee, a black tee-shirt and black running shoes. She had dark curly hair, but there was something foreign about her. Antonio was curious. He had never noticed her before.

Antonio began to watch for this woman every morning at ten. He was convinced she was not Italian – she ran alone, hair disheveled, no makeup or jewelry, loose black pants and black tee shirt. No effort to make *la bella figura.* Each morning as she ran past, he raised his cup in a salute.

"*Signora,* he would call out, "*Le piacerebbe un caffe*?"

"No, *grazie.*" She would continue past him.

Antonio liked this – a good-looking woman who was not interested in him. He could tell that she was not Italian, but he couldn't place the accent as either English or American. He needed to hear more. He couldn't very well get up and follow her. It wouldn't look right to run in a business suit, although Giacomo would have loved it. Antonio would watch as the woman disappeared around the curve past the Fontana dell'Immacolatella.

Then he would take one last bite of his cornetto and hold the tip of the pastry out for Giacomo. The Jack Russel had been sitting quietly by Antonio's chair, watching, waiting. Now was his moment. Giacomo jumped up and opened his mouth. He caught the tip of the cornetto in mid-air doing a little pirouette then sat down again very satisfied with himself.

***

Every morning Lucia would begin her day with a run along the Bay of Naples, first with her back to the sun and the sea on her left. She would run for about half an hour in this direction, passing the fishermen's dock. Just past the fisherman's dock Lucia would turn around and run in the opposite direction, with the sea on her right and the speeding traffic on her left. Now she was running toward the sun. The sea was usually a calm bright turquoise, the color of a Siamese cat's eyes.

In the morning the fishing boats were moored while the fisherman displayed their catches of the day in plastic dishpans and white enamel basins. Housewives came and bargained. The fishermen would leave by eight o'clock but the clever and frugal housewives who arrived at a quarter to eight would walk away with what was left of the catch for the price of five-thousand *lire*. Their string bags would bulge and wiggle with the flapping living fish.

In the evening Lucia would sit in the café on Via Partenope gazing at the bay, sipping a glass of red wine. This had become her habit since she had left her comfortable but grief-filled home and come to Naples.

This morning promised to be a day of grace. Just moments before at the fishermen's dock, Lucia had stopped to glance at the fish on offer. She noticed an octopus stretch out its tentacles and inch its way to the edge of the wharf, trying to make its escape into the sea. Before it reached the edge, one of the fishermen caught it. Back in the white enamel basin the octopus stayed still, sensing the fisherman's presence. When he moved away to attend to one of the housewives, the octopus again stretched out its tentacles, pulled itself out of the basin and crawled across the dock. It felt for the edge and when certain that it had found it, it pulled itself over and dropped into the sea. Lucia smiled. The octopus is an intelligent creature, she realized; she promised herself that it would no longer be a part of the seafood she consumed almost daily.

She made this vow as she turned and was greeted with approval by Vesuvius, the sun and the sea. The sun rising over Vesuvius, appearing to sit on the summit. In profile was the former Roman villa and medieval fortification Castel dell'Ovo jutting into the sea. Lucia rewarded with this perfect alignment of natural and constructed elements, the timeless mountain, the ancient castle and modern-day cars and vespas racing toward them, all illuminated by the light of the sun and displayed for her in full splendor at the precise moment she turned to face them.

That evening Lucia sat at the café sipping her red wine and thinking about the octopus. She hoped that it had learned enough not to get caught again. She looked toward her left at Vesuvius, now a dark blue bulge against a blue-violet background. The sun was setting on the right of the Bay of Naples. Half of the Castel dell'Ovo was a purple shadow, but the other half was still illuminated by the brightness of the setting sun. And Capri was outlined in the darkening sea against the red-gold sky to the right of the castle. Lucia took another sip of her wine and tried to imagine her future but could not. In Naples, the present seemed eternal.

As Antonio parked his vespa on the street beside the café, he noticed the woman again. She seemed eternally present. He started to formulate a plan to introduce himself.

On the last day of October, as was his custom, Antonio and Giacomo sat at the café on Via Partenope. As Antonio saw the woman approaching, just before she passed his table, he tossed Giacomo's piece of pastry onto the sidewalk just out of reach of his lead. Giacomo was puzzled. He looked at Antonio seeking an explanation for the change in ritual. "*Piglia*," said Antonio using the colloquial Neapolitan word for "take."

A Jack Russell terrier is very lively. He is a dog that loves a good chase. Antonio let go of Giacomo's lead just as the mysterious woman passed by his table. Out stepped Giacomo and grabbed his treat. Antonio had let go of his lead and the little dog decided that was a sufficient "go-ahead" to run himself. Jack Russell's are also talkative. Giacomo yipped and took off with the running woman. He got her attention. She was not frightened.

Not at all. She was delighted and stopped to pet Giacomo. When Antonio approached to gather Giacomo's lead, Lucia smiled.

"*Buon giorno, signora,*" said Antonio. "Do you speak Italian or English?"

"Both," answered Lucia.

"*Allora,* may I offer you a coffee?"

Lucia considered accepting his, but then she felt self-conscious about her appearance, sweating and in such inelegant clothing. So, she declined and ran on.

October had been beautiful but on exactly the first day of November, the rain started. In Naples it rains from November until May when the rain stops. Then the sun comes out and everyone goes to the sea.

But this was November and Lucia did not have an umbrella. She hated umbrellas and refused to carry one. Besides, it didn't rain constantly, only for several hours each day. Taking advantage of a break in the rain, Lucia decided to go for a walk before lunch. She didn't want to walk along the Bay of Naples today even though she had foregone her run that morning due to the pouring rain. She did not want to walk along the *lungomare* now because the sea was meant to be loved in the sunshine. She regretted missing her run. She was interested in the man with the Jack Russell, the man who would say "*buon giorno*" to her every morning as he sat drinking his coffee at the café overlooking the sea on Via Partenope, and who yesterday had let the dog run a little ways with her. She now wished she had accepted his offer of a coffee.

Lucia debated whether to walk in the dense historic center where the buildings stood so close together that they fended off the rain, and where she could stand in the Roman arcade on Via dei Tribunali if the rain got to be heavy again. Instead, however, she decided on Via Chiaia. She could always go into a café. Although she didn't acknowledge it, in the back of her mind, she wondered if that man with the dog worked or lived nearby. She knew there were offices – elegant ones –just off Via Chiaia. If you worked there or lived nearby of course you would go to the Bay of Naples to take coffee on Via Partenope while gazing out at the sea, the Castel dell'Ovo and Capri.

Lucia dressed a little differently this morning, a little more fastidiously. She still wore black pants – but slacks not running pants – to which she added her grey cashmere sweater. She added a Harris Tweed jacket to fend off the damp and a hat in case the rain started up again.

Life in Naples is unpredictable. Lucia had just reached the lion monument in Piazza dei Martiri, close to the bookstore where she had wanted to stop anyway, when the rain came again. Lucia began to walk faster and headed toward the bookstore. The rain became a deluge. Then an umbrella was over her. She looked up and saw the man, but he was without the dog this time. He had an umbrella instead.

"Signora, le piacerebbe un caffe?"

"Sí."

Suddenly, a strip of blue appeared in the grey sky and the rain stopped. Antonio furled his umbrella and he and Lucia made their way to the café next to the bookstore.

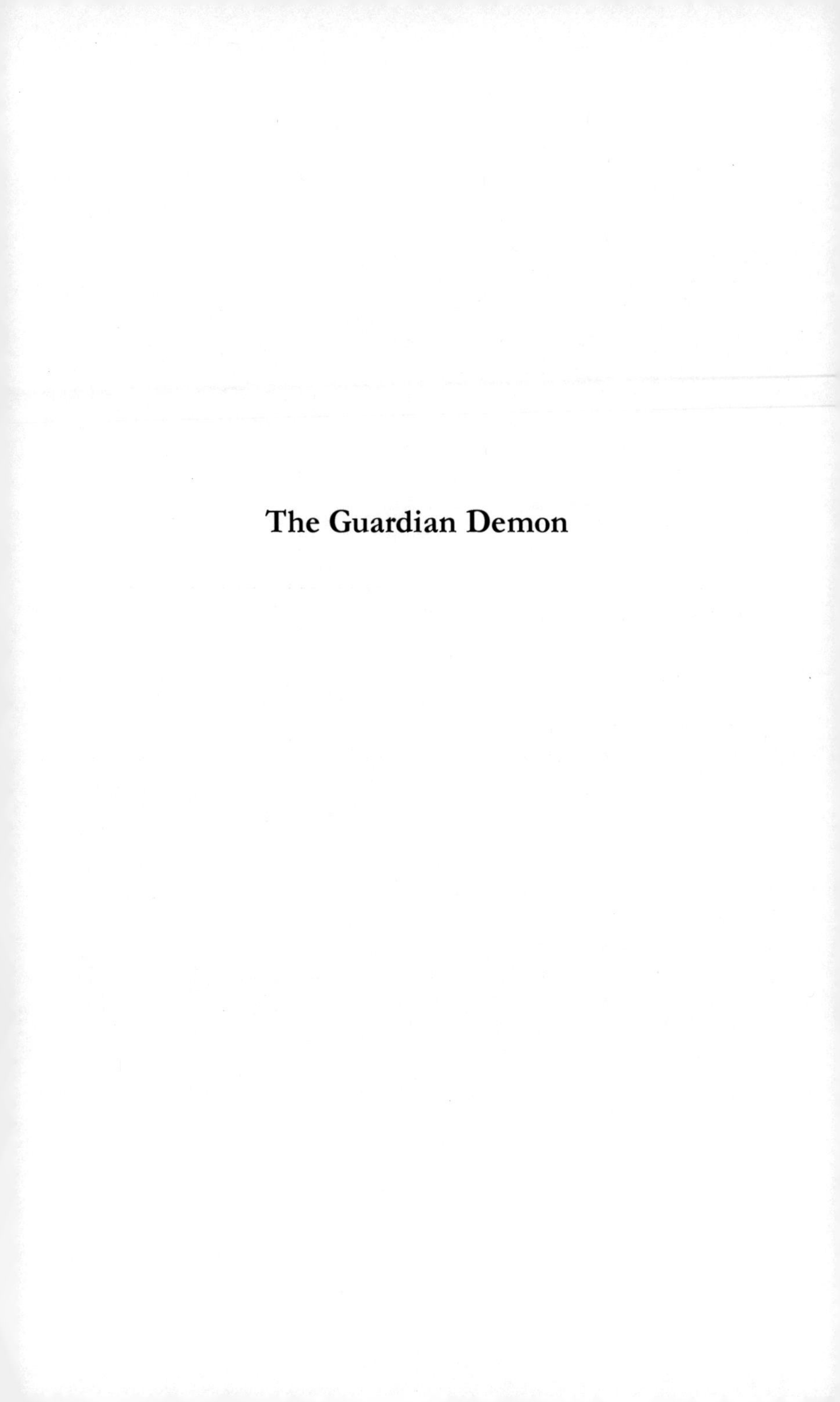

The Guardian Demon

Once upon a time there was a demon who, invisible to human eyes, roamed the streets of Naples. He could assume human shape and substance – and sometimes did – but his power, such as it was, lay more in the events he could influence. And he could hold discourse with animals.

The demon kept to places he liked, mostly the small dark streets off Via dei Tribunali. He preferred shadow to sunlight. The sun was too bright, blinding in its strength and glimmer. The sun, thought our demon, professed to reveal truth when in fact it obscured it. Shade, however, might have something to teach one. It was in the obscurity of the streets that wove through the Historic Center of Naples that he learned about love.

On a rainy Saturday, the demon Raimondo watched as a young woman hung out her laundry under the overhang of a balcony on Vico Limoncelo. She was still in pajamas and had just finished her weekly housecleaning. Raimondo understood this. He had been observing Chiara all the past week as she escorted her two little boys to school and then went to her job as a clerk in the pharmacy on Via dei Tribunali. Seeing her thus, Raimondo learned which apartment in the grand building with lion statues guarding the entrance was the one in which Chiara lived.

On Sundays Raimondo did not move about. He preferred to lurk in the shadows of the old Roman arches on Via Sapienza. He did not like the bustle in the streets of people going to church or going into pastry shops and coming out with great boxes full of *dolci* for Sunday lunch at home. He did not like the swarming restaurants buzzing with cheer of Sunday lunch out. On Sunday Raimondo kept to himself. But, on Monday morning he found himself sitting invisibly on one of the lion statues guarding the *palazzo* on Vico Limoncelo.

"Remember me," Giuseppe said to Chiara as she left with their sons for work that morning.

"Impossible to forget you," Chiara answered.

She placed a cup of steamy cappuccino and two *biscottini on* Giuseppe's carving tray. He stood up to kiss her good-by, awkwardly placing the lump of something he was working on under his blanket. He took her arm and escorted her to the door and kissed her again – a lover's kiss on the lips and told her he would make dinner, "a nice pasta Genovese."

When he got back to his chair, Giuseppe felt drained. He pulled out from under his blanket the wooden pendant he had been carving for Chiara and set to work again. "It will be finished soon," he thought. "Maybe even today."

"He's getting better," thought Chiara as she walked down Vico Limoncello. She dropped the boys at school and made her way to the pharmacy on Via dei Tribunali. As she went on her way, she thought about Giuseppe's color. It was deeper, less pale, and he smelled different. The familiar robust smell of him had returned – deep red wine and freshly carved wood. That was what

Chiara had always imagined Giuseppe had smelled of. The tired scent of illness was gone.

After Chiara and the boys had passed by, Raimondo floated up the four stories. To enter the apartment, he transformed himself into a breeze and entered her apartment through a window that had been left the slightest bit open on the side facing the street so that some fresh air might enter.

The demon Raimondo had a look around. The apartment was well-kept and welcoming. The floor in the kitchen was blue and yellow tile, clean with no cracks or chips. No dishes were piled waiting to be washed, but were arranged, still dripping, in the draining rack above the sink ready to be used for the evening meal.

He floated from the kitchen into the salon. Someone was there and that someone sensed Raimondo's presence. An old man sat by the window carving a piece of wood with delicate movement of his fingers. He stopped working and looked up when Raimondo entered.

The demon wafted around the room, looking more closely at the old man. No, he was a youngish man – very ill. Raimondo could smell how near to death the young man was. Giuseppe smiled and returned to the wooden pendant he was carving. Raimondo knew it was his gift of *addio* that Giuseppe was making for Chiara.

Chiara had begun her day feeling lighter of heart; nevertheless, a sense of something ending had crept in. There was a niche in a *palazzo* on Via Sapienza where a family she knew maintained lit votive candles in memory of their oldest son who had died in a motorcycle accident – rare in this city of skilled drivers, but it did happen. A new candle was in the niche that morning. Its flame floating in the melting wax on the top of the red glass told her that it had only just been lit. There was a single red rose – red to convey the fact that his mother was still alive – in the vase in front of Lucca's photograph.

"It's been a year," thought Chiara. "I will drop by this evening and drink a glass of amaro with Lucca's mother."

When the pharmacy closed during the long pause for lunch, Chiara went to the enoteca on Piazza Dante to buy the amaro, a fitting drink for the occasion. It was bitter, yet there was also a sense of sweetness. "Like life," Chiara thought.

She decided she would also get a liter of *primitivo* to share with Giuseppe for dinner, but the demon Raimondo had followed her and whispered to her so subtly that she believed his words to be a thought that suddenly came into her mind. "No," she said to herself, "he won't need it."

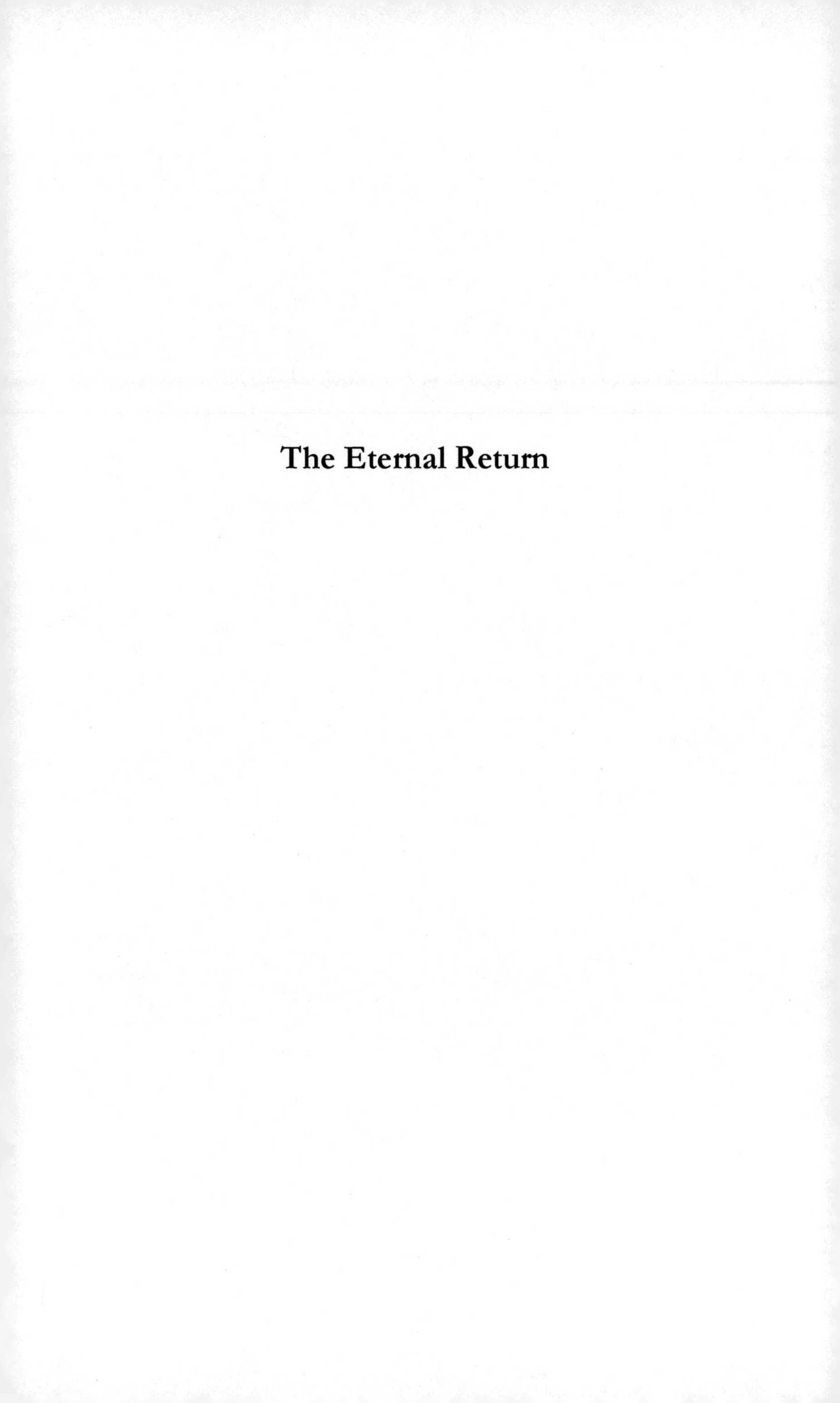

The Eternal Return

I.

Five Thousand Lire

When I graduated from university, I had the good fortune to spend some time in Naples, Italy where, of course, I studied Italian and visited all the works of art to be found in that city of visual opulence. I wasn't there alone, however. I was with my lover, a graduate student of painting and drawing. This was to have been our romantic interlude between the time of study, research and exams and the time of assuming a life of work and day-to-day responsibility. This was to have been a joyous time of fulfilled curiosity. We had arrived in May when the weather had begun to turn warm and the winter rain had ceased. This was to have been our time, utterly free.

Sometimes, I wandered the streets of Naples alone. My lover liked his solitude – he could spend hours in the Archaeological Museum sketching. He did not like learning foreign languages, so I took Italian classes by myself. It fell to me to achieve all our verbal navigation of the city, such as ordering in restaurants. I didn't mind. It made me feel knowledgeable, essential to our Italian experience. After class, in the afternoons, my lover and I would meet for coffee in Piazza Bellini, a point between the Museum and the language school. Piazza Bellini was my favorite spot where I could sit in one of the cafes for hours reading and watching the small dramas that are played out in the square. I usually arrived first.

We were a modern couple, my lover and I. We would not marry because he considered marriage a legal fiction. We had left New York to study abroad and since Naples was (in his estimation) the most artistic city in the world, here we came. I would have preferred London where I wanted to enroll in drama classes (I had been accepted), but he said that would not be fair to him – he needed to make a living as an artist and had to be where he could study and observe properly. He had to live in a city of art. So, deprived of the language of my own métier, I made do with Italian, took classes and discovered I had a feel for this graceful and complex language – and its literature.

To get to Piazza Bellini, I usually passed near the monastic complex of Santa Chiara. Outside the gates, almost every day, I would observe a beggar and his dog. The man was swarthy, with thick curly hair. The dog was a black and white mongrel, very well behaved. I noticed that from time to time, passersby would offer the animal some tidbit of food. The beggar always seemed to have lire coins in the tin dish that he proffered. I noticed that he always wore gloves, even as the weather turned from warm to hot.

Then one day, while I was waiting for my lover at a café in Piazza Bellini, the beggar approached my table. My lover was late, and I was reading – an English novel, I don't remember which. I was tired and wanted to think in my own language for a while. I was startled by the words that interrupted my browsing, the tones, in rapport with the writing before my eyes:

"If you give me five thousand lire, I will be your friend for life."

The beggar was American! I looked up, stupefied. He held out one hand. The other, gloved, he held up. The middle and ring finger of the gloves flapped, empty. His index finger and pinky were held up, palm toward me. This is the classic gesture of horns in their aspect of bringing good fortune. However, since two fingers were clearly missing, I didn't take the sign literally.

The time that it took for me to collect myself, gave the beggar the chance to scrutinize me. I could not avoid looking back. He smiled. His eyes sparkled.

"I have seen you pass on your way from the school," he said. (How did he know about the Italian school?) "I lived on Mulberry Street when I was little. After the war my family came back here."

My cappuccino and cornetto arrived, along with the bill. The waiter stood by the table, waiting for me to pay. The change included a five-thousand-lire note, equivalent to about three dollars. This was a lot to give a beggar; usually a ten-lire coin or two would be appropriate.

He repeated, "If you give me five-thousand lire, I'll be your friend for life."

Something about this good spirited bargaining called to me. I passed him the note.

I spotted him several times afterward, by the gate of Santa Chiara or by the gelato store nearby. He always greeted me, first saying – in English – that he doesn't want money; that he's fine now. Sometimes, I would pet his dog, who actually was reasonably clean.

The last time I saw the beggar was again in Piazza Bellini, in October. My lover was with me. Our time in Naples was coming to an end and the weather was turning cool. The winter rain had started, slowly, just in the mornings. Afternoons were still warm but not so much as they had been and there was a slight but unrelenting dampness underneath the warmth.

We were drinking expresso and avoiding conversation. I had suspicions that my lover had become involved with someone else and wanted to break up with me. He would not say so directly but talked about wanting to stay in Naples a while longer. I should return to the States, however.

I protested that I shouldn't be in the States right now. I reminded him that I had turned down a place at drama school in London to be here with him. He replied that I should go to London in that case; he didn't want to disrupt my plans.

My "friend for life" came up to our table. He looked at my lover and then at me. He lifted his semi-fingerless hand, palm facing the ground and moved it back and forth, the classic gesture of cheating. Then he looked at me and smiled and shook his head.

"You will be all right. Go to London," he said.

As I stood up bewildered, my "friend for life" nodded and turned his fingers downward, making the sign that protects against the evil eye.

II.

Cuma

The journey from Naples to Cuma is long – not so much in distance as in time. Cuma was founded about 2500 years ago, as a Greek colony, not far away from late twentieth century Naples where I was studying Italian and hanging out at Piazza Bellini while waiting for my lover to be finished with his painting class in the Academy of Fine Arts nearby. Every now and then, when my "friend for life" would pass by and greet me in English, made other café patrons' heads turn, for this local beggar held forth on many topics, but in the Neapolitan dialect. He also had a reputation as a fortune teller, but I think the Neapolitans are superstitious. They often mistake shrewdness and the ability to observe for supernatural powers.

There is a famous cave in Cuma where the sibyl, a prophetess, lived during the time it was a Greek colony. In those days one could visit her and ask her advice, as it was her undertaking not just to tell the future, but to offer guidance as well.

In my Italian class we had read a story about King Tarquin who had come to Cuma to consult the sibyl. She had offered him nine books of prophesy at what he considered an outrageous price. Furious, she cast three of the books into the fire and offered him the remaining six at the same price. King Tarquin again refused. So, the sibyl cast three more books into the fire. I don't know whether King Tarquin became intrigued about the prophesies the books contained or alarmed that their legacy would completely disappear, but he relented and paid for the three remaining books the price he would have paid for nine. The sibyl then vanished and so, it seems, have the books.

When I was living in Naples, there was still a tradition of visiting the cave at Cuma and asking the sibyl about the future. So, with some questions regarding what might be in store for me, I set out to find her one day when my lover said he wanted to work late at the art studio. I was disturbed by the hand gestures indicating a cheating lover that the beggar in Piazza Bellini had made over him, even though I had felt dubiously comforted by the gesture of protection the same beggar had made over me. In the back of my mind, also, was the thought that visiting Greek ruins might someday be useful for playing Medea or Iphigeneia, but where I could get such roles in Italian or in English, I had no idea.

I discovered that despite being only about twenty-five miles from Naples, it took several hours arrive at Cuma. I got an early train from the Montesanto metro station. The trains on the Cumean line were covered with graffiti, and moved slowly along the western shore of Campagna, stretching back the time as well as the distance between Naples and Cuma. More than an hour after the train left Montesanto, it stopped in a village engulfed in reeds, hot and quiet, where I walked across the track to get the bus to Cuma. I waited and waited, doubting that the bus would come, but there were other passengers who assured me that it would. Just as I had begun to believe that living in this part of the world required an act of faith that I did not have, the bus arrived. I eventually arrived at "archaeological zone" where I descended and walked to the cave.

I made my way to the center and asked the sibyl about my life with my lover. The sibyl had nothing to say to me. My future was blank. I heard a voice speaking in English, coming from the entrance. I listened. My questions remained unanswered. It was only a group of British tourists reading aloud from Virgil's *Aeneid*. They were reciting the part where Aeneas visited this very cave. The sibyl had been obliging to Aeneas. She guided him to nearby Lake Averno, the entrance to the underworld, where he descended to meet the shade of his father. Aeneas' future was foretold: his progeny would be the founders of Rome. This prediction so delicately spoken encouraged me to ask a further question. Would I have a career? But the sibyl still offered no sign. The cave was dark, cool and dry, with light pouring in through a tall odd-shaped opening at one end. I sat on a ledge and enjoyed the British reading, their clear accents reminding me of the possibilities in London that I had abdicated.

When I exited the shelter of the cave, the sun was low and the sky beginning to fade from bright blue to dusty pink. Time to return to … what? After another long wait, I took the bus back to the village. This time I did not have to cross the track for the train to Naples, but I arrived at the station just in time to miss the train. The next train was due in half an hour, but it didn't come. I sat in the station, dismayed about my lover and regretting not being in London where I would be working with familiar words, in surroundings I could understand.

There was a bar in front of the train station where three old men sat drinking coffee. When they saw me, they vied with each other to attract my attention. I saw something fly at me and jumped back. A piece of hard candy, a *caramelo*, landed where I had been standing. I glared at the old men, but this only served to delight them and they laughed out loud.

"Oh, signora, it was only a little gift for you," said one.

"Please take it. It will not harm you," said another.

"Will you have a coffee?" asked a third.

I shook my head no, thinking that forty or fifty years ago, these men had been young and strong, probably soldiers, definitely hard workers for they still looked muscular and fit. They might have been handsome. Perhaps they had been world-class seducers. Now they were just silly.

I tried to imagine my lover in the future, past his prime, talent as well as body diminished.

"No," I said aloud. "I will never know him as an old man."

The moment as I uttered this phrase, the train arrived, as though in confirmation of my statement. I did not know it yet, but the sibyl had answered my question after all.

It was night when I got back to Naples. Our flat was dark, and my lover was nowhere to be found. I noticed his easel was gone and his paint box. I opened the closet and found only my clothes. There was an envelope on the kitchen table. When I opened, I did not find the expected good-by note, not at all. There was a train ticket from Naples to Le Havre, a ferry ticket from there to Plymouth and another train ticket to London. Nothing more.

III.

The Sybil

I had every intention of using the train and ferry tickets from Naples to London that my lover had given me on his departure as his gift *d'addio*; but before I was to leave, I decided to visit Cuma again. I hoped that the Sybil had something more to tell me. I took the Cumana line from Montesanto, but instead of getting off the train at Cuma, I continued on, as if lured by the place, to the next stop at Torregaveta.

I couldn't have told you then why I was drawn here. There is a restaurant near the train station. It sits on headland that overlooks the beach at Torregaveta. Maurizio had taken me here several times for fresh mussels. Maurizio loved mussels. But that was the very reason that I wouldn't have wanted to be there. "What an affectation!" I thought as I made my way to the restaurant in spite of myself. My lover had the English name of Morris but wanting to be part of the local art scene, had taken to calling himself Maurizio.

The waters of the headland were calm and shallow, weaving around the long raspy grasses that bent in response to the breeze floating in from the open sea. Old Giuseppe was there with his knife and two empty string bags. While Maurizio sketched him, I had often watched Old Giuseppe wade in the distance until he was one with the rocks that lay at the entrance to the sea. About an hour later he would return with the bags bulging with mussels he had scraped off those rocks. The instant he caught sight of Old Giuseppe, Maurizio would shove his sketchbook and charcoal in the portfolio. The first time Old Giuseppe noticed Maurizio drawing, he came to our table and looked over the sketch. Then he dropped his bag of mussels on it, ruining it with seaweed, saltwater and black matter from the mussel shells as if he somehow mistrusted having his image captured.

***

She remembers the boat that brought her to Cuma 2500 years ago, although she had long given up counting those years. She was young then and mortal and had been dedicated by her parents to the practice of the art of divination. Being sensual, she was condemned to chastity. She had resented this. Being unruly, she had employed her gift of prophesying to counsel young lovers rather than kings or warriors. For this she was punished. Banished from the sun-drenched beaches of the Peloponnesian peninsula, she was sent to dwell in the dark cave on the marshy headland of the newly founded colony Cuma.

On the way, the boat passed the settlement of Partenope, so named for the siren that had committed suicide because she had been rejected by Ulysses. Parthenope's body had washed ashore on this spot. Be warned, Cumean Sybil!

She had been perhaps twenty years into her mortal life when she arrived at Cuma, accompanied by a crone of a chaperon. She had left behind her lover Machaon, a sculptor. Her function now would be to foretell plots against the Cumean colonists by the tribes that they were displacing. The colony throve. Her predictions she would write down in books. Centuries later, she would presage the fall of Cuma to the Etruscans. Later still, as an old woman although now immortal, she would visit Tarquin the Proud, the last king of Rome, and offer to sell him these Sibylline Books.

The boat had glided through the turquoise water that touched the shore of Partenope. It maneuvered among the headland reeds until, tangled in them, it could proceed no further. Sybil and crone descended and waded through the salt marsh to the cave. A breeze swirled around her legs like a solicitous cat and whispered that lover was dead.

***

In the restaurant I drank wine and waited a long time for my food. The waiter had appeared promptly, and I ordered a half-liter of *falanghina* and paccheri with shrimp and tomato sauce. I wasn't particularly hungry, but it seemed a shame to waste the view. I had taken a table outdoors on the beach where I could watch the sea. Every now and then I caught a diminishing glimpse of Old Giuseppe.

The wine arrived immediately. Sipping it, I watched the fishermen on the quay about twenty yards from the restaurant. They were carefully attending to that morning's catch. Every so often, one of them would walk down to the beach and return with a pail of seawater that he would spill gently over the fish flopping in their enamel basins. The fish were still alive.

The wine was working its spell. I could feel the loosening of my body beginning at the base of my neck and traveling down my spine. My shoulders were loose, but my feet didn't want to move. My body seemed at one with the gentle wind that made the waves quiver. I was aware of the intermittent whiffs of salt and fresh fish that this wind brought – a live mineral scent.

***

Now no longer mortal, the Sybil remembers the boat. Although pure spirit, she still yearns for Machaon. She was still grieving when Apollo, god of the arts, god of male beauty, god of healing, caught a glimpse of her and wanted her to be his lover. He offered her immortality and she accepted. Apollo granted her immortality, but not eternal youth, so she aged and withered until she diminished entirely. Only her voice remains, carried on the wind.

The breeze today is like that of long ago, but now the Sibyl and the breeze are one. Someone, she is aware, is here to seek counsel about a lover.

***

Mentally I drifted off to London. I would soon be a part of the theater scene there. A line from a play by Harold Pinter floated through my mind: "There are some things one remembers even though they may never have happened." "Morris," I murmured and wondered if the Sybil had put that thought into my head.

I was startled to see my waiter approach from the direction of fishermen's quay with a bowl of shrimp that would soon become my lunch. One fell from the bowl and out of nowhere there was Ciro, the cat that lives at the restaurant. His nose was twitching, his ears lay back. He watched for a few seconds then turned his back to the fallen shrimp, pretending not to see it. Then he made a swift leap and scooped the shrimp up with his paw. This is mouse-hunting behavior. He has learned well. With the shrimp in his mouth, Ciro looked around, deciding upon a secluded dining spot. He chose to go under a table near my own but surrounded on two sides by the wall of the restaurant, with an open view of people (and other cats) coming and going.

***

When the wind whispers, the sea listens. The diver sensed his name in the movement of the water. He speared the fish swimming nearby and began his ascent to the surface. He was pleased with his catch, a fine orata of unusual size that would bring a fine price at the restaurant on the beach. The diver suddenly realized he was hungry. He would have his usual feast.

Old Giuseppe heard the whispered words and smiled – at least it was as much of a smile as he ever gave. That spirit who lives in the cave is at it again he thought.

"Allora, buona fortuna." *he muttered to himself.*

He noticed something dark moving in the water and looked down. It was the diver making his way to the surface. Then Old Giuseppe understood. He scraped one final colony of mussels off the rock, forced it into his bulging string bag and began his swim back to the restaurant on the beach.

He had seen that woman there alone, probably feeding her lunch to that beggarly cat. The man who usually came with her was noticeably not there. 'Meno male," *he thought.*

When the wind whispers, the earth listens. The sand moved with the breeze forming undulating m's.

The sound of mmmm carried on the breeze and the woman heard it whisper the name of her former lover.

***

"Michele Merisi, Michelangelo Merisi." Caravaggio? Morris's favorite artist whose name was really Michelangelo Merisi. But it was Maurizio; it was Morris. He was the lover who left me. Oh, Fate! Save me from artists.

Finally, my paccheri arrived, topped with freshly cooked shrimp. I put a piece aside to cool and extended my hand to Ciro. "Come here."

The cat looked puzzled. I repeated in Italian: "*Vieni qui*."

Ciro installed himself under the chair next to me. The waiter lovingly refilled my glass.

I thought I saw Old Giuseppe returning. No, it was someone else, a stranger out of the sea. He was wearing a wet suit and in one hand was carrying flippers, while in the other dangled an *orata*. This fish is two feet long! That's twice the length of the *orata* you find in the fish market at *Sanitá*. I stared while the stranger passed his fish off to the headwaiter whose eyes lit up at its size.

The stranger then ordered linguini with mussels and disappeared. I forced myself to focus on my paccheri but was still not particularly hungry.

The stranger returned a few minutes later, having changed out of his wet suit. He took a table near mine and requested a bottle of *fiano*, a very good white wine from this region, be brought to him immediately. The bottle the waiter brought was obviously well chilled, dripping with condensation. I noticed that the waiter also brought two delicate-looking wine glasses – tulip-shaped with an etched border.

Ciro was still under my table. What a ragamuffin of a cat – white stomach and legs, striped back and muzzle and a long raccoon tail. I slipped him another shrimp while the waiter was back in the kitchen. The stranger noticed and smiled. I thought it might be a smirk.

There was a portfolio on the floor beside the stranger. Where had that come from? He probably had an arrangement – a place to change his clothes, a fish that he had caught purchased by the restaurant. He poured himself a glass of wine from his well-chilled bottle, opened the portfolio and withdrew a tablet and charcoal and began to sketch.

I turned away and saw Old Giuseppe returning, his two string bags stretched to the limit with mussels. A feast for tomorrow night after they have been cleaned thoroughly to remove the sand. Some will be eaten raw; some steamed with garlic and butter; some will be cooked with tomatoes and herbs. All will be accompanied with linguini lightly coated with butter and garlic. Ciro will be disappointed. He cannot eat the remains of mussels. He prefers shrimp.

I pushed the paccheri around on my plate and slipped some more shrimp to the ragamuffin Ciro. He gobbled it up, but then went to the stranger and rubbed against his legs. Then this man from the sea filled the second glass and offered it to me.

"My name is Michele," he said. "Will you please share a glass of wine with me?"

I accepted and introduced myself. As we touched our glasses together in a toast, I noticed that dusk was coming on. The waiter lit two large torches at either end of the restaurant. Immediately I noticed bats circling in the distance, catching the evening's insects before they had a chance to seek cover. I imagined these bats have just emerged from the Sybil's cave close by.

I wonder if I were the Sybil in a former life, punished with recurring mortality for betraying my calling and giving myself to a lover. I have seen my lover's powers of destruction. I know there is also the power of creation.

Acknowledgements

This book would not have been written without my husband Jim Mauro who once made the outlandish suggestion that we spend a year in another country learning another language. Nor would it have taken shape without the New York Writers' Coalition and the writing workshops I attend regularly.

I would like to thank my friends in Naples, the women of the American International Women's Club (and their husbands), who helped me know the secrets of the city; the friends I made through the Italian School, *Centro Italiano*; and Valentina who first opened the door to us.

I am also grateful to my Italian teacher in New York, Mariella Bonavita who has encouraged me to write, and to all the friends, too numerous to name here, for all the encouragement and support that they have offered. Nothing can come to fruition without that.